Social Animals

Species

Addison Fulton

Copyright © 2024 Addison Fulton

Published Exclusively and Globally by Far West Press

All rights reserved. No part of this book may be reproduced in any form or by any electronic or mechanical means, including information storage and retrieval systems, without written permission from the publisher or author, except in the case of a reviewer, who may quote brief passages in a review. Scanning, uploading, and electronic distribution of this book or the facilitation of such without the permission of the publisher is prohibited. Your support of the author's rights is appreciated.

www.farwestpress.com

First Edition

ISBN 979-8-9887354-8-9

Printed in the United States of America

"wild women don't get the blues"

-Ida Cox

There is a rabbit. It's across the quad; Anna doesn't see it, but Correy sees it and hears it and feels its presence like a broken tooth. Across the quad, a few yards from the overly chlorinated fountain and the other students milling about, there is a rabbit with its back to Anna and Correy.

"And the thing is, I just can't decide if it's worth it, you know? Like, it's pretty, sure, and I do like it! But it's *so* expensive." Anna has a picture of a dress that is supposedly the cola-cherry red she has been seeking open on her cellphone, which she presents like communion wine. Correy can't bring herself to take a sip or offer an in-depth opinion. She wants to be helpful, but she doesn't have Anna's particular eye for color; the nuance between cherry and wine and blood red is lost on her. And, there is a rabbit across the courtyard. It has turned its head toward them, lifted onto its haunches like it's on the verge of sprinting. They are walking towards it.

"Uh-huh," Correy agrees, eyes on the rabbit.

Rabbits become atypically bold when they start to become accustomed to human presence.

In that way, they are like dogs.

A rabbit, however, will never eat out of the palm of your hand. In that way, they are unlike dogs. Correy would know.

"I'm just sick of wasting money, you know?" Anna continues. "So, I don't want to buy it if I *don't* think I'm actually going to wear it because that's just wasteful."

"Right."

It's not as though Correy thinks that rabbits are somehow more cowardly animals than dogs, domestic or wild. She's not *judging* them. Correy's always thought that felt unfair to the rabbit and reductive to the canine. They just have different fears. Rabbits are afraid of all sorts of things that humans and dogs aren't afraid of: humans, dogs, hawks, all sorts of sounds...

"I asked Derren if he thought I should get it, and he said that I should 'do whatever I wanted', which isn't helpful at all because I don't *know* what I want."

...Cars, Correy adds to her mental list of 'things rabbits are afraid of'. That one's understandable, she thinks as she opens the passenger door of Anna's red car; Anna could probably name the exact shade, but all Correy can say is that it's red and it's a car.

And that a rabbit would be afraid of it. She's not afraid of it, or at least, she thinks she isn't as she climbs into the passenger seat.

"I think you should get it," Correy says after Anna has turned the ignition. Their destination is technically within walking distance, but Anna prefers to drive. The rabbit sprints out of sight. "I like it."

"I don't know," Anna says, biting her lip in worry. "We'll see."

Both dogs (at least the domestic ones) and humans are afraid of doing the wrong thing. Correy would *know*.

Rabbits probably aren't afraid of that, and maybe that makes them braver animals than canines or humans; it would certainly make rabbits braver than Correy, who is both human and canine.

"I'm not buying it," Anna decides when they stop at a red light.

"Why not? It's pretty."

"Too expensive."

It was pretty, Correy thinks. She wasn't certain about her reds, but she knew pretty.

At least, she's pretty sure.

The building that houses Anna and Correy's shared dorm is one of the newer buildings on campus, so there is no ivy creeping up its side. Its exterior is a cool gray concrete with sharp, perfect corners and clean lines, brutally modern and modernly brutal. Anna, with her sharp eyes for design, loathes it.

"It doesn't fit with the look of the rest of the school," She'd explained once. "Everything else has got the warm brick and oak wood style. It just doesn't work."

Anna likes everything to fit together, Correy has learned. As an extension, Anna wants everything she likes to fit together.

"Is Jamie gonna be there tonight?" Correy asks as they climb the stairs to their room in the building Anna hates. Correy wants to hate it too, a little, as an act of solidarity. It is ugly. But, one of the benefits of a modern building is a better heating and cooling system, which Correy cannot find in her heart to hate.

"No. Not tonight, it's not his scene. And he has a chem quiz tomorrow and he wants to study. Lame."

"Oh…"

"Yeah."

"Derren will be there though. He's meeting us there."

"Oh."

"Yeah."

Jamie is Anna's old friend from high school. Anna can call him lame only because they are friends, and have been for such a long time. Anna and Jamie, it seems, have very little in common. He bites his fingernails and stays up late to work on advanced problem sets; he gets this glazy, frightened look in his eye when he speaks sometimes. Anna keeps her nails painted, is a good driver, and laughs at the right volume for the right amount of time. Correy's mother would like Anna. Correy likes being Anna's friend. She thinks Jamie likes being Anna's friend too, though Correy doesn't understand why. Jamie and Anna do share a common species, which should count for a lot but counts for very little, and a common history which counts for a lot. Correy shares neither. It is important to Anna that Correy and Jamie be friends because Anna likes the things she likes to like each other. Correy and Jamie are friends, most likely.

Derren is Anna's boyfriend and Correy hates him. She knows Anna likes (loves him, even) him, and she wants so badly to not hate him. She wants to not hate most people. She can't, though. She just can't. He smells too strongly of a cologne Correy can't stand, and has a constant knowing smirk that grotesquely twists a mediocre-at-best face. He isn't nice. Correy has tried liking him; it felt like trying to swallow a wishbone.

"That's too bad, about Jamie," Correy says.
"Yeah, I know. But it'll still be fun."

Correy alone is granted the privilege of being in the bathroom while Anna gets ready. Derren always meets Anna at the event in question; he never comes to their dorm early. Jamie, on the rare occasion he ventures into the social scene, often joins them ahead of time, riding in Anna's red car there and back. Anna likes and trusts Jamie, but he is still banished from the bathroom during the sanctified 'getting ready time'.
It is only Correy.
"It's a bonding ritual, you know?" Anna explained, then asked for Correy's opinion on which of two lipsticks was better. Correy remains proud that her lipstick opinion had been the correct opinion; Anna had applied it, then grinned, bearing all her teeth and asking if she'd gotten pigment on any of them. She hadn't.

Now, the bonding ritual remains unchanged, Anna plucks between her eyebrows as Correy brushes her teeth and watches her friend out of the corner of her eye. Normally she wouldn't be so wary, but tonight is a full moon and Correy is a werewolf.

She'd never bothered to explain the whole "lycanthropy" thing to her peers. She wouldn't even know where to start. Whenever she imagines talking about it, she can't imagine actually saying the words, "I am a werewolf."

Her mother says it's because she's ashamed. Correy isn't certain that's it, she thinks the sentence just sounds clunky. Plus, it's just odd. Correy often forgets other people don't just know she's a werewolf. She's known it since she was born. There is a lot humans get wrong about werewolves. For instance, her wolfishness was inherited; she got it from her mother. Lycanthropy is a recessive gene and Correy very well could've just been a human, like her father was. She just got unlucky.

The wolf transformation isn't immediate, either. It's gradual, subtle. It starts in her teeth, the aptly named canines, which elongate and ache. She brushes them carefully and watches Anna making sure her friend doesn't notice her fangs. Her mother so badly wanted her to have human friends, and she didn't know how Anna would react.

"Shit!" Anna curses suddenly and Correy jumps, the plastic toothbrush nearly slipping through her grip.

But Anna isn't looking at Correy, she's staring at her own reflection in the mirror, staring at a little bubble of blood beading between her eyes like a red car in a parking lot. It shines, round and bright in the bathroom's harsh light. Is blood really blood red? Or is it more like cherry? Anna wipes it away with a tissue carefully, sighing.

"Pulled a hair too hard," she explains, tossing the tissue away. "Pretty hurts!" Then she picks up the tweezers again.

"Pretty hurts," Correy echoes, smiling without her teeth.

Turning into a wolf is like hunger; by the time she can feel it in her belly, she's already there. But, if she's careful, she can make an appearance at a frat party per Anna's request and still slip away into the cover of stunted desert trees and open desert night before anyone notices, spend the night chasing rabbits, and be back in the morning when she's approximately human again. She can go out tonight, and everything will be okay.

"Thanks again for coming tonight," Anna says with one last look in the mirror. "These things are always much more fun with you."

"Oh, of course! Anytime!"

Correy, since she could not truly (permanently) be a person, had settled on being a people-pleaser.

)◯(

The frat house is within walking distance of the dorms; not even Anna could justify driving. That was okay with Correy, it would arguably make sneaking away even easier if Anna wouldn't be expecting to give Correy a ride home. Everything was going to be okay.

"Plus, it means we can both get drunk!" Anna had added as they walked.

Everyone is drunk on something. Correy, for instance, is drunk on the smell of sweat and heat and closeness, a haze of human pheromones that permeate from every pore of every person crammed into a closed space. She is drunk on camaraderie, on the dim lights that hide her strange teeth, on the fantasy that she will not have to slip out the back very soon. She is drunk on being human, if only for a little longer.

She is also drunk on simple, standard-issue cheap beer.

Next to the drunkenness, starting to stir is that hunger feeling. She can feel it in her throat; it makes her speech even slower than alcohol would. Growly and hungry and a reminder that she has to leave. She should leave now.

"Correy?" She hears Anna call from somewhere in the crowd. It's not the first time tonight Anna's called out, not the first time Correy has not responded. She slipped away deliberately earlier; it's a bad friend thing to do, but it means that Anna won't follow her; she won't know where to look. Anna will look for her where a human should be, not where a wolf is. That's how it has to be.

She should leave now.

"I should leave now," she says, or at least she thinks she says to the strangers she stands by. The music is loud enough to drown out her voice, even as her ears get more sensitive, more animal. She abandons her cup on a table and starts to head for one of the doors that leads outside.

"Hey, hey... Where are you headed off to so early?"

Correy's path is blocked by a nameless wall of humanness, complete with the smell of sweat and alcohol. Too intense. Humanity is less cute up close. She shoves past, opening the door and forcing her way outside. The human follows her.

"I need to leave."

"Come on, the party's just gettin' started," says another human at her back. They hunt in packs, she knows this.

"I need to leave," she repeats, continuing further

away, hoping they'll get tired and give up. She doesn't stop walking but doesn't start sprinting yet either.

"What? Not having fun?"

"I need to leave," she says again. It's all she can think to say.

"No, I don't think you should leave, not until my friend and I can show you a fun time."

Then they both laugh.

One grabs her by the waist and pulls her impossibly closer to himself. She yelps and twists and his grip holds. *It is not uncommon for a canine caught in a trap to bite off the ensnared limb to escape but there's no gnawing off the hip bones–*

Then, Correy starts to understand the rabbit.

Then, alongside fear and haze and drunk, hunger fully blooms.

)O(

Growling. No longer in warning. In summoning. From acid, from the lining of the stomach, from the hunger at the heart of the thing. Hunger which is as much in the heart as the rest of the guts. As the brain. No more rabbit. No. Maybe more rabbit. More teeth. More hunger. Love and fear and reverence are in the passenger's seat. Hunger drives. Maybe love and fear and reverence are hunger. Questions are stomached, swallowed, stowed away for the cold season.

For now, there is meat.

Meat that is frozen. Unused, perhaps, to its own fight or flight response. Used perhaps, to be the apex predator.

Not tonight, tonight it is meat.

Teeth which ached to do their job are indulged. Muscles bound to pounce are indulged. Emptiness indulged. Hunger indulged. Leporidae indulged. Canidae indulged. The moon watches. Only the moon. There is squealing, but no scattering. She is not joined or interrupted. Distantly, a heartbeat. Steady, then, unaware. No sense in chasing, no sense in running. Focused, then, on the feast. Wet. Warm. Stringy, sweet. Soft, no feathers, no scales, little fur. Rare meat.

Rare meat.

New to the consumer. New to the consumed.

The stomach of the body is satiated. The stomach of the heart is not. The teeth are not. Clamour still then. Urging, rarely met.

Tonight is new, the hunger old.

Only the moon. Only the distant collective heartbeat.

Only the moon. A distant, singular heartbeat.

"Correy?"
"She probably left already. Let's just go."

Only the moon. Only silence.

Then the sun.

)O(

Correy wakes the next morning, approximately human, next to a dead actual human. She remembers next to nothing. She remembers being cornered and scared, then being cornered and angry. Nothing on *her* body hurts, save perhaps a tenderness around her nail beds and the ache of her fangs receding.

Probably nothing *hurts* on the body of the guy beside her. Nothing hurts because he's dead. Because he's dead. He's *so* dead, and Correy killed him. She's sticky with sweat and blood. She's going to be sick. Desert dust clings to her skin and she wants to shake and scratch until she feels clean again, feels *human* again, but first, she has to deal with the body.

There are deep teeth and claw marks lined with red, shimmering, and gaping in the rising sun. It doesn't look like a murder, it looks like an animal attack. She did that because she is an animal and when somebody wakes up and comes outside and finds her all soaked in blood they will put together what she did and everyone will know and they'll call the cops and animal control and she'll spend the rest of her days in a cage if they don't decide to just put a bullet in her skull right then and save themselves the trouble and maybe they'll cut open her brain and check for rabies but they won't find rabies they'll just find–

Calm down, she orders herself, trying to play both the handler and the animal. *Calm down and think.*

She hasn't been found yet; there's still time. The frat house is smaller in the distance. She is surrounded by hard dirt, small trees, and large rocks. She scrapes her foot through the dirt; it's scratchy and well-armored. She can't bury the body here.

The body.

She can't leave it where it is though, in view of the fraternity's house. Her hands are numb with dread as she grabs the body by the arms and drags. One finger is broken, the bones crushed by her jaws. She drags it behind two rocks and covers it with branches snapped off of brittle trees. She can't bury the body here, but she hides it like she's intending to come back and finish what she started. She is intending to come back.

Her stomach churns at the realization, curling defensively in on itself. She needs help.

"Correy! Sorry I lost you last night. I looked for you, but we had to go eventually. I–," Anna freezes in the open doorway as she processes the picture before her. Anna's eyes are dark and shiny. When they're hit by the early sunlight streaming in through the windows, they glow from within, a deep and healthy shade of brown like the earth you *could* bury a body in.

Correy is still covered in blood and desert dust.

"I'm sorry I disappeared. I couldn't find my key this morning," Correy confesses, as though that's the worst of it.

"Are you okay?" Anna asks. Correy doesn't know how to answer that. She thinks *she's* okay. Something terrible had very nearly happened to her, but it hadn't. She'd done something terrible though. Was she okay?

"I need your help."

"Yeah. You look like it. Wait, that didn't sound right. Just with that– I mean, yeah. What happened?"

Correy's stomach flinches again, trying to escape her body via her spine. She can't just say what happened. She could pretend she found that frat boy (whose name she didn't know, had he known her name?) just the way he was, mauled by some animal and hidden behind a rock, but Correy was covered in the blood. It won't make sense. She could pretend she'd killed him as a human, but Correy is (was?) an animal. It won't make sense.

She's going to have to tell Anna.

She has no choice. If she tries to deal with this alone, she'll get caught, that's for sure. And Anna... Anna is her friend. She'd help her. At least, Correy thinks so. Believes so, perhaps naively, that Anna is as loyal to Correy as she is to Anna. If she's not...

Well, then, Correy is doomed anyway. But she trusts Anna's steady hands and keen eyes. If Anna chooses to dispose of her, at least she'd make it humane. They're friends.

"Come with me?" Correy begs. "And don't ask any questions until I can explain?"

"What's up?" Calls someone Correy can't see from the doorway. Her stomach gives up on fleeing and decides to just lie down and die inside of her.

"I should've mentioned," Anna says with a wince. "Jamie's here."

Jamie appears in the doorway. He is wearing his glasses and noticing the viscera and dirt that Correy is covered in. He swallows. His hands shake.

"I'm sorry. I need your help," Correy repeats.

"Okay, okay sure. Do you want to take a shower? Get clean first?"

"No."

"Okay."

Jamie accompanies Anna, either because morbid curiosity has won out over fear, as it often does, or because he believes, however ironically, in the safety of a pack. Correy leads them both to the rocks and hasty branch pile where she hid the man she killed. Jamie only stares at the dead human, face suddenly pale. Anna glances at it, then at Correy, then at it, then at Correy again. She has never felt less like them.

"I'm sorry," She repeats. It's like she's forgotten the rest of human language entirely. Correy stares at the ground that isn't bloody.

"Did you... do this?" Anna asks.

Correy nods, still not looking at her friends, only the earth.

"Well, we have to get rid of it, right?" Jamie says. Correy's head snaps up. "We can't just leave it, someone will find it and your DNA's probably all over. Unless this happened without um... touching him?"

Correy tore those holes with her teeth, "There's probably DNA."

"Okay, so what we'll do is we'll dissolve the body

in acid and–"

"Where are we gonna get *acid*?" Anna demands.

"I don't know! It's just the best way to get rid of organic–"

"Why do you know that?" Correy asks, startled out of her silence.

"Why did you kill someone?!"

"Jamie!" Anna hisses.

"Sorry, bad question."

"It's okay," Correy says.

"Is it?" Jamie asks.

"Focus," Anna reminds them all before Correy can answer. "We need to get rid of it, we have no acid."

"We bury it. And then we disappear."

"Okay," Correy nods. She smiles, hysteria bubbling in the wake of her fleeing stomach. It'll be gone, everything will be okay.

"No, we can't do that," Anna says.

"Why not?" Correy could cry. Please, just let it be done, just get rid of it and make it all be over so she can go back to pretending–

"Because people saw us, saw you at the party with this guy..." she gestures at the corpse. Her nails are long and smooth and tipped in white polish. Correy's nails have blood under them. Jamie's nails are shaking. "...Was last seen alive at! If you disappear, it'll look weird."

She has a point.

"So we bury it, and we come back," Jamie says.

"What?"

"Were there any witnesses?" He asks Correy.

"I don't..." Correy barely remembers it. Her brain had literally been smaller; trying to recall her own actions from the night before feels like watching a slasher film through a pinhole. A pinhole that moves erratically and constantly with no relent or focus. Everything is red and hazy. Were there?

Witnesses? No screaming. Just... snarling and yelping and whining. Just one? Had to have been. "No. No witnesses. Just him."

"Well..." Anna says, "So, if no one saw you, and there's DNA evidence..."

"And none of us act suspicious or nervous..." Jamie continues.

"Well, more nervous," Anna teases.

"Time and place!" Jamie huffs.

"Sorry."

"If none of us act *weird*, then no one will suspect us, and then–"

"Everything will be okay," Correy concludes.

They are going to drive as far north in Anna's red car as they can go before it gets too dark. Jamie hopes to cross a state line, thinking it'll make the body harder to find or trace to them, but that's negotiable. What matters is north. North gets more rain, the ground will be soft and diggable.

"There'll be worms, too, to help with the decomposition," Correy had added. Jamie had flinched.

"That's good to know. How, uh, how do you know that?"

When they'd loaded the dead human in the back of Anna's red car, Jamie had accidentally stuck his hand into one of the gashes in its chest. He doesn't seem to be Correy's friend anymore. He's scared of her because she'd put those gashes there.

"My mom likes to garden," Correy snapped. "This is my first time killing someone."

"Okay!" He puts his hands up in surrender, "I'm sorry, I just wanted to be sure."

It didn't feel good, being scary. Not to her at least,

maybe to humans, maybe to the de—

Correy didn't finish that thought. She still hasn't finished that thought. She keeps her eyes on the blur of trees as they drive north, shadows growing longer as they continue, north, north, north.

"How did you do it, anyway? With a broken beer bottle, or..?"

"Jamie..." glaring at the passenger seat he occupies.

"Sorry, sorry! You don't have to answer that, just curious."

Now would be the time to tell them. They couldn't exactly tell anyone else, without revealing how they knew and thereby admitting they'd helped Correy cover it up. She cracks her window open a bit. The breeze tears through the silence. The trees move in a blur, rapid and soothing like the turning of the earth. The air is pine. If there were ever a time, now would be the time to tell them.

"I'm a werewolf. I did that with my teeth. And some of it with claws, probably."

"Okay fair enough," Jamie sighs. "Ask stupid questions, get stupid answers."

"I'm not trying to give you a stupid answer," she insists, "I'm telling you the truth! I'm a werewolf," Correy was right, it was a stupid sentence to just say. Not shameful, just stupid.

"You can let the joke go now."

"Not a joke."

"So, what then? You're telling us you're actu–"

"I believe her," Anna cuts in.

"You believe her?"

"You tell me how else that happened, you said it yourself Jamie, while we were in the gas station–"

Correy had not been allowed to go into the gas station to buy road snacks with cash and go to the bathroom. She'd still been covered in blood. She's still covered in blood, it makes her stick to the interior of

Anna's red car.

"–That an *animal* had done it."

"I said it *looked* like an animal did it! Important distinction! Because an animal couldn't have done it, because, unless you've *forgotten* one *really important thing*," Jamie's voice edges towards hysterics; Anna presses the accelerator. "Werewolves aren't *REAL*!"

"Yes, they are," Correy counters quietly, aiming for de-escalation and landing on gasoline as Anna presses the red car harder, faster. There are no longer trees outside, only green and blurriness.

"Why lie? And last night was a full moon. Lines up. Plus, there's this big dog that I see sometimes outside my dorm window and I thought maybe it was a lost pet or some wild animal with distemper, but apparently, it's just Correy. Who's a werewolf."

"It was me, I'm a werewolf."

"You're not! You're crazy! Both of you are! Your... your guilt is driving you insane!"

"You know Jamie, maybe you're crazy! Maybe you–"

Then Anna yelps as Jamie yanks the steering wheel out of her hand. She slams the breaks which squeal and bleed rubber all over the asphalt.

"What the hell was *that*?!" Anna demands, "You could've killed us!"

Correy understands though; there was a rabbit. They were careening towards it in their little red car and it was frozen on the road.

"There was a rabbit," Jamie explains, "I didn't want to..." He trails off.

"There was a rabbit," Correy agrees.

Jamie nods, then twists, curling in on himself in the passenger seat, away from Correy and Anna, protecting his vulnerable spots and staring at the window instead of looking at either of them

"Correy's a werewolf," he concedes.

Near sunset, Anna remembers that Correy is covered in blood.

"We should get that off of you, huh?" She says. "And your clothes?"

"Probably," Correy agrees. "It might be a little incriminating."

They're driving through the streets of a small, sleepy, and sunburned town. The stop signs are worn down to a fleshy pink by the wind, the light, and the dust. They've encountered one stoplight, the red light also raw. The town, however, has the last pay-to-use laundromat in a 50-mile radius. So for now, they stayed.

The top edge of the laundromats is rimmed in flickering blue neon, the most saturated shade for miles. The linoleum was once white, someone is making a valiant effort to keep it pristine, but still, dust and shoes and time have left their mark; the edges of each tile are tinged with yellow, like teeth.

Correy wears a brand-new navy hoodie, the sleeves of which are not quite long enough. She tugs at them, and they recede up her arm. She tugs again, and they recede. She can't find it within herself to complain though, Anna had gotten it for her. And she only has to wear it until the clothes in the washing machine are clean.

"Do you think just detergent will be enough to get blood out? And the DNA?" Correy asks.

"How would I know?" Jamie asks. "And keep your voice down."

Jamie's admission of Correy being a werewolf did not make them friends again. Neither had their brief moment of mutual understanding with the rabbit.

Anna had left them in silence when she went into a small town store to buy the navy hoodie that's a little too small.

"Why can't I come?" Jamie complained, still curled away.

"You don't know fashion," Anna said, that teasing lightness in her voice. "You'll be a bad influence."

Anna laughed; no one laughed with her.

"Fine," Jamie says. Correy had nothing to say.

"I'll be back."

Jamie and Correy sat in long silence. He curled away from her. She picked at the blood under her nails.

Anna returned with items in plastic bags and saw Jamie and Correy were exactly as she had left them.

"I got baby wipes," she said. Correy took them, reaching out, at last reminded her that her body could still move, if willed. "For the, ya know..."

Anna gestured to her face and arms. The baby wipes are for the blood Correy was still covered in.

"Thanks," She started by cleaning the blood under her nails.

"I grabbed this too," and Anna produced the navy hoodie that Correy now wears in the laundromat. "It was the best thing they had," she explained, then to Jamie, she said, "You could've come with, it's not like you could've made the options worse!" She tried to joke.

Jamie was silent.

Jamie is still silent in the laundromat, watching bloody clothes spin around and around, slowly coming clean. Neon hums.

"I hope so," Correy says after a few more circles from the washing machine.

"Me too," Anna agrees. Then she sighs. "And it's a

laundromat in a small town right next to a Motel 6, this can't be the first time someone's come over to get blood out of clothes."

"Or worse," Correy says.

"Or worse!"

"Still," Jamie argues, his voice dropping to a whisper, "We should be careful. After all, you killed someone."

Correy yanks on the hoodie sleeve again to try to cover her pulse point and doesn't respond.

"Hey! Speaking of Motel 6, I'm gonna go see if they have any vacancies and if they take cash. When we're done, I don't think we're gonna wanna just sleep in my car. Oh, shit! And I should clean the car. I'll be back."

"Wait! You can't–"

Both Jamie and Correy reach to stop Anna from leaving, but she is gone.

The sun is under the horizon now, though its dissipating light lingers like DNA may or may not linger on clothing. The dusk and the neon make Jamie's skin blue. He fixes his glasses with shaky hands and watches the washing machine go around and around. There is an empty seat between them where Anna had been sitting. Correy watches him.

"Can you please stop staring at me?"

"I'm sorry."

"It's okay."

"I didn't mean to scare you," she didn't, *honestly*.

The washing machine chirps a cheery tune, indicating it's done the best it can. Jamie opens it before Correy can get there. He inspects the shirt collar. In the blue, the blood isn't blood red or any red. It just looks dark, harmless.

"Not quite," Jamie grumbles. "Maybe one more wash cycle."

He pours more detergent and throws the shirt

back in. They try again, around and around in soap bubbles and blue.

"The werewolf thing... Does that only happen on the full moon?"

"Yeah."

"Why?"

Correy had asked her mother the same question when she was young.

"That's just how it is," Correy says, repeating her mother's words.

"So you're not going to turn into a wolf in like... seven minutes?"

"No. Why seven minutes?"

"That's when the sun will officially be set."

"Oh."

Blue. Around and around.

"If you do turn into a wolf again, do you think you're going to kill someone else?"

"No, I hope not. I don't think so."

"So even if you were a wolf right now, you wouldn't kill me? Or Anna?"

"No."

"Why did you..." He gestures to the washing machine, where they are washing away the human's blood.

Why *did* she? She hadn't been thinking. She just... did. Instinct.

"I was scared. And then he grabbed me. Then I was angry, then I was a wolf," she says, "You know how animals can get when they're scared. We do dumb things."

Jamie stares more, frozen.

"So, they kind of deserved it, then. Didn't they?"

"I guess," Correy shrugs.

"I have a scar from where my sister's hamster bit me

because I picked it up wrong when I was little," he says at last and holds out his shaky hand and shows her the half-moon silver of off-color skin. It looks like a river under the neon.

"I didn't know hamsters could be so vicious," Correy admits.

"I guess anything can be if you provoke it."

"Even humans?" Correy asks.

"I mean obviously–"

"I'm not human. Not really," she reminds him begrudgingly.

"Well, technically, but you are... I mean..." He can't finish his sentence so he coughs, instead. The washing machine finishes its cycle.

"I think we got it out," he declares, and he smiles, his teeth blue like he's been drinking laundry detergent.

)O(

It is time to bury the body. Crickets murmur in the darkness, which makes Correy squirm and scratch compulsively at sticky phantom blood behind her ear.

"You think this is far enough?" She asks.

In addition to the hoodie and the baby wipes, Anna had purchased several gardening kits made for children, which include tiny plastic shovels with ladybug patterns.

"I thought adult shovels would look suspicious! Now I just look like a sad stressed-out single mother of three instead of someone who's..." her voice drops and she glances around, making sure none of the crickets are listening to her close enough to hear her continue "... Someone who's hiding a dead body."

Anna has a great point, but digging a frat-boy-sized body with child-sized ladybug shovels eats time. It's exhausting. It's dark. The crickets chatter on.

"I appreciate the cover story," Jamie says, "I really

do. But could we have gotten slightly bigger shovels?

"I'm *sorry*," Anna snarls. "I was stressed!"

"It's okay," Correy says. "We can do this, everything will be okay."

"Shit!" Jamie's ladybug shovel has been decapitated, its plastic neck snaps in half and splinters.

"Here," Correy says, passing her shovel to Jamie. "I can just use my hands. I'm pretty good at digging. Go figure."

Jamie and Anna laugh, bubbling like rabies spittle around their mouths. Correy loves it, a little bit.

She drags her fingers through soft dirt. She pulls away small roots, but no worms. Immediately, the space between her nails and the flesh of her fingers is dirtied again. It smells healthy and alive. She is surrounded on all sides by dark, rich, greens. Jamie and Anna talk and dig with ladybug shovels, but it becomes background noise like the crickets. Correy breathes deep and strong and fast. She is wild and delighted.

For a moment, she forgets she is digging a hole to hide the body of a man she killed. Time passes; she moves dirt with her hands.

"Do you think that's deep enough?"

"Yes. It should be"

"Hey, Correy. You can stop digging now."

Her head snaps up and she blinks. Her friends are dark shadows.

"Let's grab him," Anna says. Jamie cracks his knuckles and his shadow nods. Correy climbs out of the hole they've dug.

"Watch your hands," Jamie reminds them. Jamie grabs the dead human's head and tilts his head toward the stars to avoid looking at its face. Correy grabs the torso, watching her hands. Anna holds the corpse's feet.

Could Correy have done this, hiding the body on

her own? She wonders. The unmarked grave she could've dug. It might've taken her a bit longer, but she could've done it. The body, though? Maybe not. It takes about two and a half humans to clean up one wolf's mess.

"I think that's it. I think we did it," Jamie exhales, and Correy copies him. Relief and pine and movable dirt fill her nose.

"We did it?"

"We did it!"

She could cry. She could scream with joy.

"Then we should go," she says instead, and they pile into Anna's red car and drive out of the woods.

"I wonder if we're the only people currently staying here that just hid a body."

"Jamie!"

"What? It's a serious question. Just, statistically speaking."

"We can't be the only ones," Correy offers.

"We can't be!" Jamie agrees.

"You guys are freaking me out," Anna complains from the bathroom. She's wiping her face with one of the newly acquired baby wipes. "But... if we're talking about motel murder suspects, I'd definitely say the guy in the three-piece who was leaving just as we came in."

"He was so creepy!"

"You don't think *he* saw *us*? Do you?" Jamie's spine straightens, and his eyes flick to the door.

"No, he was too busy talking to *somebody* on the phone."

"Definitely a burner phone, right?"

"Oh definitely," Correy nods.

"Who do we think he was calling?" Jamie asks, leaning

forward.

"Getaway driver?"

"Accomplice!"

"Victim? To lure them out?"

"Oh, maybe!"

Anna's phone rings where it sits on the sink.

"It's Derren," Anna says with a sigh. Then her eyes widen, bright. "Shit! I didn't tell him where I was going to be this weekend. Maybe I need a burner phone," she laughs nervously. She holds one nail between her teeth, not chewing, just gripping.

"Hey Derren," she says. Anna can't hear Derren's voice on the other line. Anna's hand moves from resting between the tip of her teeth to resting on the back of her neck.

"Sorry... Yeah..." Anna says. She rolls her eyes at her friends.

Correy and Jamie glance at each other. Correy doesn't like Derren.

"It was a... family emergency," Anna's hand returns to her teeth.

"I didn't think you'd want to... I know. I should've called you... Okay... I'll be back on Monday. Sunday evening, probably. Alright. Love you... okay. Bye."

"Is he mad at you?" Jamie asks. "Is he onto us?"

"No," Anna says. Her voice has an airy shakiness, "No, he believed me about the family emergency thing. And he wouldn't care to check to make sure it was true. Plus he doesn't like my family very much. We're fine."

Jamie nods.

"Are *you* okay?" Correy asks.

"Yeah, I'm fine. I mean Derren and I argued a little, and we're probably gonna argue about it more, but it's nothing serious. We have little fights like these a lot."

Both Jamie and Correy nod.

"He's a good guy," Anna insists. "He just doesn't

like being out of the loop. That's all. I should've called him."

Stillness.

"I'm gonna take a quick shower," Anna says. "Let's see if the soap gives me a rash."

That gets a half-hearted chuckle, but the group is quiet for the rest of the night.

)O(

Correy wakes hungry. From the woods where they buried the dead human, birds sing and giggle. No policemen bash down the door of their motel room.

"Is anyone else hungry?" She asks the others.

Jamie, who offered, no, insisted, on sleeping on the floor lifts his head from his makeshift pillow created by balling up the recently cleaned clothes from the laundromat. They'll need to be cleaned again, Correy thinks. Motel floors are not notorious for their cleanliness. That's okay. Better safe than sorry.

"Yeah, actually," he says. "Starving."

He squints his eyes, fumbling around the scratchy carpet for something.

"They're on the nightstand," Anna reminds him, voice groggy and growly but warm. Her face is still stuffed in the pillows. Correy hadn't even realized she was awake. Anna half-heartedly flails her arm out, pointing in the direction of the nightstand which held what Jamie was evidently looking for. His glasses, Correy realizes when he picks them up.

"Thanks," he stands, stretches, long and sinewy, and slips the glasses on. "We should get breakfast before we go."

"I don't want to..." Anna whines, pulling her blanket over her head again. "I'm warm. I'm comfy. You get food, and you bring it to me."

"Absolutely not. Get up," Jamie says.

Correy would've done it, she realizes with a start. She'd have gone and killed one of the lovely little songbirds from the woods and brought it back if it made her friends happy. She owes them; she'll owe them forever. It'd be how she says 'Thank you'.

"Alright," Anna sighs and throws the blanket off of herself. "Let's go get breakfast. I saw a diner on our way into town."

The diner is filled with sunlight and quiet chatter. Other humans sit around, nursing cups of coffee and plates of bacon. She and Anna sit on one side of a vinyl booth, with Jamie on the other. The smell is sweet and overwhelming. Correy bends one of the plastic-covered menus away from her and listens to it crack back in place. The offerings are the same offerings that exist at every human diner, everywhere in the world. Humans are so predictable to each other; they can guess other humans' breakfast choices and set them in stone. Or... paper covered in crinkly-sounding plastic. They have done a good job. Jamie orders a vegetable omelet and breakfast potatoes and a cup of coffee. Anna orders a Greek yogurt parfait with seasonal berries and granola. Anna is frozen, staring at the menu. She is starving. Jamie and Anna are waiting.

Eventually, she orders a plate full of bacon and eggs, because it is at the top of the menu.

"That'll be all?" The waitress asks.

"Yes," Correy answers.

Food arrives fast and polite. This, Correy understands, is a good diner. Anna comments on the lack of roaches and asks if Jamie is relieved.

"Are you ever going to let that go?"

"No, no I'm never gonna let it go. You screamed like a baby, it was hilarious!"

At Correy's confused look, Jamie explains, "One time we went to breakfast in *middle school* and a cockroach ran across my pancakes, and Anna thinks that egregious health code violations are *hilarious*, apparently."

"It's hilarious when you squeal, literally *squeal*."

"I did not *squeal*, okay? And no, no roaches this time, thank god," Jamie says, cutting into eggs and vegetables and biting down, which reminds Correy that the smell of salt and sugar and grease that fills the space is in part coming from the plate in front of her. Food; that she should eat.

She picks the bacon up first. It's warm and gritty beneath the pads of her fingers. The fat pockets are wet and slightly slimy. It's undercooked. Pink, veiny, fleshy red streaked through with silvery white.

She bites down and feels warmth and meat explode on her tongue. Immediately, her stomach roars to life. It's delicious. She feels sick. She's *starving*. She bites down again; this bite is crunchier. She feels her stomach surge upwards, whether it's to meet the fried pork halfway there or to escape via her mouth, she can't tell. Is she sick? Or is she starving?

At the third bite, she gives up. She thinks it must be making her sick. Maybe she should go vegetarian, maybe the bacon is too close to what she's done. Sick is better than the alternative, that the bacon is too close to what she has done and she's *still hungry*.

The eggs go down smoother. They are fluffy, well-done, savory, and easy, except for where bacon grease has touched them.

Anna takes another spoonful of Greek yogurt, her head twisted to the side, "Well?" She asks Correy, "What do you think?"

"Huh?"

"Would you eat a bug for 100 dollars?"

"Oh, sorry. I wasn't paying attention."

"That's okay," Jamie says, "You seem pretty focused on your eggs."

"They're good eggs."

"Yeah, they're not bad for middle-of-nowhere diner eggs," Jamie agrees.

"The bacon isn't very good, though," Correy comments. "It's kind of raw."

"We're getting off-topic," Anna reminds. "Would you eat a bug for 100 bucks? I would. Jamie wouldn't because he's a coward."

"Hey!"

"It depends on the bug," Correy says, "I think if it was too mushy I couldn't."

"So you'd rather eat one with a shell? Like a beetle?"

Correy thinks about a crunch beneath her teeth giving way to wetness, the innards of an unlucky bug coating her mouth.

Like bacon, but worse.

"No... Nothing with a shell. Maybe I couldn't eat a bug, I think I'm with Jamie on this one."

"Thank you."

"You're both crazy. You just swallow it fast and then you're 100 dollars richer! I'd do it. So long as it wasn't a poisonous bug, I'd be okay. And 100 dollars richer."

)0(

There are no police cars on campus when they return. Correy had imagined the whole place would've been locked down, with red and blue flashing lights and a sea of college students with pitchforks ready to hunt the monster themselves.

But the campus so far seemed normal. As though nothing had ever happened. Maybe no one had noticed. Maybe no one had even noticed the frat boy missing. It couldn't be that uncommon. Correy always wanted to know where her friends were and be with them if possible, but Correy wasn't human. Maybe no one had noticed yet.

They'll notice soon, snarls that fearful voice. She felt it more in her stomach than in her head, cooling pools of dread like grease. *But even if they notice,* she reminds herself, *you'll be fine. You buried it. Everything will be okay.*

"I should go see Derren," Anna says. "He's been texting me a lot. He wants to hang out."

"Oh, that's okay," Correy says, "We have to be normal, right? And seeing your boyfriend is super normal. So..."

"Yeah, so I'm gonna do that."

"Sounds good," Jamie says, "Normal."

"See you later?" Correy asks.

"Yeah, see you later!" She chirps, then she heads out, door closing behind her, leaving Correy in their shared dorm room with Jamie.

"I can't–"

"I can't stand Derren," they say in unison.

Maybe a walk would clear her head. Correy was twitchy, feeling caged on all sides by walls and ceilings. No one on campus had given any indication that they knew what she'd done, yet she'd become convinced that even if the people didn't know, the buildings knew. The buildings knew, and they wanted her out because they were built for humans and knew she wasn't one. Or maybe they knew she wasn't human, so they wanted to lock her far away from the humans they were built to protect; they'd come to life and chain her to one of their radiators just like the werewolves in the old horror movies.

Maybe a walk would clear her head.

The wind was half-hearted at best, picking up both the dust and strands of Correy's hair, then immediately putting it back down, without much tousling or shifting. Perhaps it was tired, perhaps it hadn't slept well. The sun was relentless, warm, and unblinking, a singular star in a cloudless expanse. It had so much space and time to account for. At least the moon had some company. At least the moon took one night off, every now and then. Correy wondered if the sun hated the moon. She wondered if she hated the moon.

The campus was built into the ridges and hills of the desert. Correy picked one, one of the taller ridges, and paced along its length, watching human life unfold in the valleys below her.

A blonde man on a skateboard rode over a reddish-brown rock that was too large to be swallowed by the wheels and spat back out again. He recovered, arms flailing for balance before his knees hit the asphalt. The skateboard moved a little ahead of him, then stopped, ever patient in waiting for his human companion.

Anna was with Derren. Jamie had a computer science class.

The man with the skateboard glanced around, checking to see if anyone had seen him almost fall off the board. The various students around the quad had, in fact, seen him fall off the skateboard yet when the skateboard man looked at them to ask, they suddenly became immensely enamored with the bricks of the older buildings or their own shoes or the sun.

Humans, as a side-effect of being a notoriously proud species, were conscious of not offending each other's pride. The skateboard man assumed no one had seen him and remounted his skateboard with the severity of a cowboy who'd been shot in the gut remounting a faithful horse. Perhaps a Western would fit better than a horror story. Correy could be the loyal cattle dog.

Anna was with Derren. Jamie had a computer science class.

Two people who had watched the skateboarder fall had been sitting on a bench. Now, one of them stood and gestured for the other to join them. She did, but first, she had to double back to throw a paper cup into a waste bin. She recycles it. Then, at an awkward half-jog, she rejoins her friend who is waiting for her. Together, they start walking towards their destination, which is in the opposite direction as the waste bin. They are talking, but Correy can't hear what they're talking about. The one who had gotten off of the bench first kicks the red rock that the skateboarder had tripped over, and it skids across the pavement. Perhaps that was an act of revenge and an act of solidarity with the skateboarder. Humanity, standing together against the tyranny of stones. Perhaps it was simply for the joy of kicking a rock, watching it bounce, hearing it knock and scrape against concrete. Humanity, in its never-ending quest to find joy. Correy isn't sure.
She kicks a rock of her own. It is more of a yellow-brown than a red-brown. It does not bounce or make a cool sound, because she kicked it across dust, rather than concrete.

The walk has not cleared her head. Anna was with Derren. Jamie had a computer science class.

She climbs off of her ridge and takes one of the

many paths back to her dorm. Anna would have driven her. She is walking on the opposite side of the street and in the opposite direction as a man who did not shave that morning and is walking a dog. At her approach, the dog rears on its leash and yelps, barking and pulling.

"Comet!" says the man, pulling the dog back. The dog continues to strain and yelp. "Down, girl!" Her tail is wagging.

The dog, Correy realizes is pulling to say hello to her. The man who did not shave this morning does not want his dog to say hi to Correy, but the dog is stronger than the man. Comet the dog, in her innocent and animal excitement, succeeds in dragging him off of the sidewalk and into the narrow two-way road; Comet pulls despite the man's protest until she reaches Correy.

"I'm sorry about her," the man says as the dog leaps to put her paws on Correy's stomach. "She's not normally like this."

The man doesn't want to look her in the eyes. She looks at his short stubble instead.

"That's okay," Correy says, honestly.

"She's normally pretty well-behaved," the man elaborates.

"Uh-huh."

"And shy."

"Uh-huh."

"I'm not sure what's gotten into her," he concludes.

"It's okay," Correy says. "Dogs tend to like me," she explains.

"Oh? Are you a dog person, too?"

Vaguely, Correy wonders if he realizes the enormity of what he has asked. He isn't a werewolf, she knows with certainty. Her father wanted a family dog, her mother said that they already had two.

"I don't think of myself that way," Correy answers.

She is not a person, or a dog, or a dog-person. She is something else entirely. She is so different from the man who did not shave that morning in ways he will never be able to comprehend. Comet has removed her paws from Correy's tummy but still looks up at her, tail wagging. "Dogs are cool, though."

Correy is in the library with Elizabeth from biology class on Tuesday night to study together for a test the next morning. Elizabeth has mascara on her eyelid, smudged over her nude eyeshadow. Elizabeth is good at biology. She has the next book open in front of her, smudged mascara eyes roaming over the text.

"Sexual selection is the process by which certain traits are propagated and continued through a population through sexual desirability. Mates are chosen based on desirable traits. While it has a similar end result as natural selection, ie, the improvement of the species via organisms with beneficial traits passing on their genes, it fundamentally diverges. Whereas natural selection is a matter of only the strong surviving, sexual selection is a matter of–"

"Only the pretty survive?"

"Basically! Well, technically, only the pretty mate... Which I guess is kind of the same thing. In the evolutionary sense. I don't know."

Elizabeth from biology class would know, probably does know. She's good at biology. Correy is fascinated by biology, though she isn't certain she'd call herself good. She must not be awful, or else Elizabeth who is good at biology would've found another person to study with. The order of the stages of the Krebs Cycle and mitosis come easily enough, though what *happens* at each stage is another question. Correy's good with scientific names, too. The whole interest had started with an endeavor (ongoing) to classify herself into some species, genus, and family. It led Correy to being, as far as she knows, the first werewolf to go to college. She's the first in her own family, at least.

She majored in ecology. She hopes she's good at biology.

"I just worry you're barking up the wrong tree," her mother had said when Correy had told her the plan. "I mean, you want to find a taxonomical denomination of werewolves? That's not going to help us, hon."

"I just want to know what I am, *really*."

"You're my daughter," her mother said. "And you're a werewolf, like me. And like your grandmother."

But Correy still wanted a scientific name.

"I think we're going to be fine," Elizabeth says, closing the heavy textbook. "We just have to remember that things that help you survive and help you find a mate also help your genes get passed on and help your children survive. And that's the goal of every species."

"That sounds good. That makes sense."

Does it make sense? Is that the goal of her species? She supposes she wants to survive. Is she a good animal? Did nature do a good job with her? *Should* her mother have passed on that gene?

"So, how was your weekend?" Elizabeth asks. Correy startles, shutting her book with a jolt. *She doesn't know,* Elizabeth reminds herself. *There's no possible way she could know, you were so* careful...

"Oh, you know, sort of boring. Didn't really do anything. I, uh, went on a hike," she says.

"That's fun!" Elizabeth says. "Yeah, I didn't do anything. I mostly just studied and watched TV, which was nice."

"That sounds good," Correy says. "That sounds relaxing."

"Yeah! It was. I thought about going to that party at Beta Kappa, but I didn't. Those kinds of parties always creep me out a little bit. Not really my scene."

Beta Kappa sounded familiar.

Correy swallowed a bout of nervous laughter that burned on its way down, "Yeah. They get... a little wild."

"Did you hear about those two frat guys who are apparently missing? Crazy, right?"

"What?" Correy's shock was sincere. Not that it had happened, but that Elizabeth from biology had heard about it, and that... "Two? Missing?"

"Yeah, I know!"

"Wow..."

"They're probably fine, right? I mean, probably just sleeping off a hangover in some motel room."

"Probably," Correy agrees. There were two of them. Correy had only buried one. Where was the other?

She still remembers very little of that night. She remembers meat beneath her teeth. She remembers flesh and anger. How much flesh? Only blurs, her memories moved too quickly to count, to classify one moving, squirming creature. She might as well have been chasing her tail that night, had she not woken up to one dead human beside her. But two had been missing. That meant she had a witness. Someone saw her and ran.

"Crazy," Elizabeth says again, "What some people get up to on the weekends."

"Yeah," Correy echoes again. "Wild."

An article in the school's newspaper, the *Daily Explorer,* (named after the school's mascot, which was inspired by the explorers who had pushed the boundaries of American cities ever westward) confirmed that not only did the students know about the two frat guys who were missing, but the police knew about it as well. Correy was furious that she only could remember one frat boy who was missing. They were looking into last known locations, speaking to families, friends, and people who had seen them most recently. They were speaking to the people who had seen them last... as in... most likely people who had been at that party.

The party that Correy had been at.

The party that Correy had only killed one human at. She read on.

At last, Correy learns their names: Tyler and Colton. Tyler's face she recognizes. It was looking up at her when she woke up beside him. It was looking up at her with glassy eyes and a gaping hole in his chest. She recognized his glassy eyes looking up at her from a grave dug with two plastic ladybug shovels and two of her own hands.

Colton is the one who got away from her. In his student ID picture, he has a smile on his face. He has perfectly square and human teeth.

Correy has never been so frightened of anyone. More than that, more than the fear of discovery that sits in her human-esque mind, fresh rage sits in her animal stomach.

No one will know what he knows, her stomach mutters, *if you got to him before anyone else did. You could put him in the ground. Then no one would know, and everything would be okay.*

"Hey, how's it going?" Anna says. Correy hadn't heard the door unlock, she'd been too absorbed in a college school newspaper.

"Hey," Correy replies with a jolt, flipping to the Arts and Media section of the magazine. She doesn't know what she's hiding from Anna, who already knows everything.

"Anything interesting?"

"The cops know that Tyler is missing," Anna confesses.

"Tyler?"

"The... the frat guy. Who we buried in the woods."

"Oh," Anna sits by Correy's side, glancing over her shoulder. She flips back to the article discussing the case.

"Okay, they say missing, not *dead*, which is good."

"Missing might as well mean dead."

"That's true..."

"It says two people are missing," Correy says. "We... I..."

"Maybe it's unrelated? Just... a guy who went missing?"

"Maybe," Correy agrees.

"There's no reason for anybody to suspect that we were involved in any of it, okay? There were a ton of people at that party. And no cops have bashed our door down. Yet."

They sit together in uncomfortable silence, waiting for irony to grab them and strangle their hopes. Someone in the dorm above them takes their shoes off; they both flinch at the soft sound. But then there is quiet.

"Do you think we're going to get caught?" Correy asks. Then she squeezes her eyes shut, shakes her head, and clarifies. "Do you think that *I'm* going to get caught?"

"No," Anna says immediately. "No, we were careful."

Correy nods. She wants to believe her.

"And, just so you know... if we do get caught, which we won't, it would be us who get caught. You know that, right?"

Correy tilts her head and feels her eyebrows scrunch. She doesn't understand.

"I mean, like, I'd also... take the fall with you. You know? I was technically abetting. But I also wouldn't let you, like, go to jail on your own. We stick together."

"Really?"

"Yeah! Maybe they'd even let us be roomies in prison!" Anna tries to laugh, then seems to realize it isn't funny. Correy appreciates the attempt anyway. She's a pack animal.

"Thank you."

)◯(

Correy had gotten an 83 on the biology test she'd studied for with Elizabeth and had not been contacted yet by the police. That was a good sign, a sign that she and her friends had successfully acted normal so far.

Correy's phone rings and she jumps, the trap of fear closing on her heart. *Spoke too soon.* But the caller ID is not an unfamiliar one: it's her father.

"Hi, Dad," she mutters. Normally, she looks forward to these calls with her father, but today there is so much she can't tell him.

"Hey, Correy!" He says, eternally enthusiastic. "How's school?"

"School's fine. School's good. I got an 83 on my biology test."

I murdered someone last week, she briefly contemplates saying, *I tore someone to shreds with my bare teeth, and I got an 83 on my biology test. Are you proud of me? Are you disappointed?*

"How's home?" She asks instead.

"Oh, fine," her father says. Home is usually fine. "The most recent yield of tomatoes was small. They were good! But there weren't very many."

"Do we have worms?"

"Mom thinks we do. She also thinks the soil is bad. I told her, I told her the later harvests tend to get smaller. The plants are near the end of their life cycle, I say. She doesn't believe me though, you know how she can be. She thinks we can squeeze a few more tomatoes out, that we usually have a few more good weeks of tomatoes, usually."

Correy nods, then remembers that her father can't see her, "I know."

Mom is obsessive about her vegetable garden. It's hard to coax growing things in their backyard, the soil is too dry; they are too far inland for the Pacific to help them.

"Can't hurt to check for worms," Correy says. They get worms a lot in their tomato plants. There is so little that grows without cultivation, so the worms have few other options for food sources.

"It's late for them."

Tomato worms are not, in fact, worms the way the body-eating earthworms were. Tomato worms are, in fact, caterpillars. They turn into hock moths, or sphinx moths when they reach maturity. They hang around flowers, drinking nectar and mating. Then, the female finds a plant to lay her eggs on so that her babies can eat the plant while they wait to become moths. It is late for worms, they should've become hawkmoths by now. It was one of the cycles that Correy knew from biology.

"It's been warm lately."

Maybe the warmth had delayed the worms' pupation. Maybe the longer-lasting heat had allowed the initial worms to reach maturity and produce more worms of their own. If *that* were the case, the second generation of moths would have particular trouble finding flowers to drink nectar from and mate on.

"Possible," Her father says, "I'll check."

When Correy was still home, she would help deworm the tomato plants. Her mother refused to do it. She told their father that it was a fear of the worms, of general bugs; Correy knew that wasn't true. Her mother was not afraid of bugs. Once, when her father had to travel for a business trip, it had been just her and her mother in the war against the tomato worms and the moths they became. Mom had squashed a moth against the window with her bare hand and impossible animal speed.

"Don't tell your father," her mother had instructed her with an urgency like she'd killed something far larger and more important than a tomato worm turned hawk moth. What her mother was afraid of was looking gross.

"We made marinara sauce with the tomatoes. It's good," her father says to Correy through the phone.

"That's good."

"We have a lot left over."

"You can use it again, that's good," Correy says.

"Yeah! We can," her father said. "We could send you some too if you wanted. Jar it and ship it to you."

"That's okay. I have the dining hall."

"You sure?"

"I'm sure, thank you, Dad."

The moth her mother had murdered was trying to reach the light above the kitchen table, which it could see through the window. Moths used the moon and the stars to navigate; they got disoriented and confused by the non-natural lights, which was why they tried to fly to them. Telling as much to her mother earned the moths little pity.

"I'd rather they fly to the moon than try to fly into our kitchen," she'd said. Correy pictured it, small, furry brown bodies adjusting to new gravity, trying to find a way to orient themselves now that their previous navigation point was below their six little feet. Trying to find tomato plants on the moon. Her mother cleaned the dead moth off of the window with glass cleaner. The next morning she showed Correy how to cut the worms in half with just her fingernails. Then, Correy had copied her technique of getting worm blood out from under her nails as they washed their hands side-by-side. In the motel, she'd tested if the same technique was cross-applicable to human blood. It was.

Her mother hated the moon; she didn't want either of them to be werewolves.

"Got any plans for this weekend?" He asks her.

"No, not yet. Maybe just studying."

"You should get out this weekend. College is one of the funnest times in your life. Are you having fun?"

I killed a man and buried his body last week, Dad. I think his friend saw me. Is that fun? Is that the human college experience?

She bites her tongue to stop herself. It's not kind, it's not necessary, it's not smart.

"I am," she says instead. "Maybe Anna and I will do something this weekend if she doesn't have plans."

"Anna... Anna... do I know her?" Her dad asks.

"You do. You met her. She has the red car and the French manicures."

"I do know her!" He sounds delighted. "That sounds fun."

"Okay, I'll ask her."

"Okay," her dad agrees. "I gotta go now. Love you."

"Love you too."

Correy presses the end call button and glances out her window. The sun is beginning its descent. She wonders if there will be any moths by her window tonight; she wonders if any moths ever have made it to the moon.

Probably not.

Anna did have plans that weekend, as it would turn out. She and Derren were going to get drinks that night at one of the bars near campus. It was known for its dim and smoky atmosphere.

"On weekends there's live music," Anna had said.

"That sounds fun," Correy said.

"It sounds loud," Jamie countered.

"It's funny you should say that," Anna said, intentionally directing the next part to Correy and turning her head away from Jamie. "It isn't like a date *date* so if you guys want to come, it might be more fun. Derren said it was fine. We're finally at the 'meeting each other's friends' stage. And I think it'd be fun if you guys came. *Both* of you guys."

"I think that sounds fun," Correy said, she remembered the creak of her desk chair as she leaned forward.

"No," Jamie says.

"Please?"

"I have a paper!" He insists.

"Come on," Correy says. Ordinarily, she'd let Jamie do whatever he wanted. Let any human do whatever they wanted. She surprises herself, almost. "It'll be more fun if we all go. After everything? Can we just hang out like normal friends? Please?"

"Like Correy said," Anna agreed, "Please?"

Jamie is silent for a moment; he chews on his shakey nails in contemplation.

"Fine," he says at last.

Now, Correy regrets her boldness and her insistence. The bar is smoky, as advertised, but Correy realized quickly she does not like smokey. The live music is also there, as advertised. It is bad live music. Correy's pretty sure it isn't just that she doesn't like it.

Jamie hates it too, whispering as much to Correy. She nodded, crushing a handful of complimentary nuts beneath her teeth. Maybe this was a mistake.

Correy has also forgotten how much she hates Derren. He, much like the bar, is smokey and loud. He greets Anna first and wraps his hand around her waist from behind in a way that makes Correy's stomach twist. He plants a flat, wet, way too long, and way too loud kiss on her cheek.

"Hey baby," he says right by Anna's ear, voice wet and sludgy like an old puddle, more oil and algae than water. "You look good."

"Hey, Derren," she says. She angles her head slightly, moving her ear away from his mouth. "This is Correy," Anna says, gesturing to her.

Correy waves, a little scared and a little angry.

Derren smiles, frightening and infuriating. His teeth are very white, glowing in the dim and smoke.

"What's up?" He asks.

Correy doesn't know.

She smiles in return, rather, bears her teeth and hopes the question is rhetorical, the way human questions often are.

"And you remember Jamie," she continues.

"Yeah! I remember Jamie!" Derren unwinds his arm from where it'd sat around Anna's neck to approach where Jamie sits. "How ya doin' man?!" He asks, and he punches Jamie on the arm. Jamie flinches, curling into himself, away from Derren and toward the wooden bar and the complimentary mixed nuts.

"Please don't punch me," Jamie requests.

"Ah, this guy," Derren says, slapping Jamie on the back instead. "Scooch," he instructs Correy, who sits by Anna. There's an open seat on the other side of Anna.

Correy scooches.

Derren presses another kiss to Anna's cheek, she

laughs and shoves him a little, only barely still playful.

So, babe," the word sounds slightly unnatural on Anna's tongue. "How was your day?"

"Good! Better now," he says, nuzzling into her neck. "I've been looking forward to tonight."

Anna laughs again, nervousness bubbling through.

"Bar-keep!" He snaps his fingers in the air, grabbing the attention of a tired-looking woman in low-rise jeans.

"What can I get for you?" She asks.

"Yeah, I'll just do a beer. Chilled. In a bottle, not a glass. Something dark. And she'll do tequila with fresh lime juice. Got that? No lime syrup. No limonade. Just a squeeze..." He demonstrates, squeezing an invisible lime, "...Of fresh lime juice."

The barista glances at Anna to confirm. She nods, and the barista nods back.

"I'll do a rum and coke?" Correy asks like it's a question.

"Okay," the barista says.

"Yeah, okay," Derren scoffs.

"That's not funny," Anna says, quietly.

"I'm not saying it's funny!" He looks Correy up and down and says, "Good choice."

He reaches for the nuts in front of him and tosses an almond into his mouth. He misses it. He tries again. This time he succeeds and chews it with his mouth open. He grabs a toothpick and starts to remove the remains of almond flesh from between his teeth.

Is she being made fun of?

"And you?" The barista asks.

"I don't really drink," Jamie says.

Derren scoffs again.

"Pussy," he says. He takes the toothpick out of his mouth and drops it on the bar. There's spit on it. Correy is the only one who heard what he said. Anna is listening to the bad live music, her attention rapt but her face grimacing. Jamie is explaining to the bartender why he doesn't drink. He does drink, but not tonight. Not a lot though, when he does drink. This goes on. Correy is glad he didn't hear.

"Could I please get a lemonade, though?"

"Can do," says the bartender. "Should I open a tab for you guys?"

"Yup," Derren said, grabbing a macadamia nut. This time he just eats it, not bothering to toss it and catch it.

"Awesome. That'll be right out," The bartender flips her little notepad closed and turns away to start gathering alcohol and mixers and lemonade.

"God, look at the ass on her," he says, leaning over Correy to direct the comment to Jamie, who says nothing, staring with wide eyes from behind his glasses, jaw functionally wired shut. Derren doesn't seem to notice or care.

"I'd like to see that shaken not stirred, if you know what I mean," Derren offers a fist bump to Jamie, who offers a minute shake of his head and keeps his hands in his lap.

"I don't know what you mean," Jamie says.

Anna laughs harsher and sharper than Correy's heard it before. "Derren, come on..."

"What? It's just a joke, babe. Chill." He grabs a fistful of the nut mix, shoves it in his mouth, and says through his spit, "Take a joke."

"I know it's a joke," she laughs, uncomfortable. "I'm just saying, time and place."

Derren raises an eyebrow. Correy watches Anna's throat contract.

"You're right," she says. "I'm being dramatic. You're just having fun! We're all just having fun, right?"

"Right!"

"Right," Correy and Jamie agree.

The group lapses into silence again. Anna, now,

reaches for the small glass bowl. She grabs a handful, then picks through it, extracting and eating one at a time. The band playing bad live music on the stage has finished and is packing away guitars and picks. The drummer stumbles standing up from his drum kit. Another band replaces them and starts playing different live music. Correy can't tell if she likes the new music better, or worse, or the same. She thinks her favorite music might've been the drummer quietly apologizing to the drum kit he'd gotten tangled in. She likes to imagine the drums had also apologized.

Their drinks arrive around the time Anna has finished picking through her small handful of nuts.

"Finally," Derren says, with another one of his scoffs.

The cola is syrupy and the rum is warm. Anna tips her head back towards the bar's dim lights and downs the tequila with freshly squeezed lime juice in one moment. Jamie stirs the lemonade in small circles, the ice clinking against the glass.

"I'm trying to see if I can make a tornado," Jamie explains to Correy quietly. She nods. Anna is muttering something to Derren. He sighs and takes a swig of the beer that was brought to him in a chilled bottle.

"So, Correy, right?" Derren says to her.

Correy nods.

"What's your major?" He asks, voice dull and flat.

"Ecology," She says.

"That's like plants and animals and shit." His voice does not tilt up at the end, the way Correy is used to humans doing to indicate a question. She answers anyway.

"Yeah, that's the basics of it at least. Life cycles and things."

Anna is smiling at her.

"I'm a business major," Derren says. "It's pretty

tough."

Correy nods. Anna is still smiling at her. Jamie is still trying to make a tornado.

"That's cool," she says.

Anna reaches for another handful of nuts; Correy copies her. She has reached the bottom of the rum and coke.

"Maybe you should lay off the nuts a little, babe," Derren says to Anna, not caring that the others hear, "You don't want to end up like…" He angles his head toward Correy, who feels strange shame roar to life in her stomach, wriggling like a worm next to the familiar roaring and scratching of anger.

"'Nother round?" The bartender has returned to ask.

"Yes, please," Anna says.

"Yeah," Correy follows, "But could you make it with Diet Coke this time?" She thought maybe that would rebury the shame worm; it doesn't.

"It's the wrong viscosity to make a tornado," Jamie says, referring to the lemonade. He says it in a whisper like they're in on a secret together.

"That's sad," Correy says, genuinely.

"I know," Jamie agrees.

"So, Jamie, do you just never drink? Like ever?" Derren asks.

"I do. Sometimes. Just not tonight. We need a designated driver."

That's not true, Correy knows. They didn't take Anna's red car today because Anna intended to spend the night at Derren's apartment. They walked.

"But sometimes, yeah," Jamie says. He picks up the lemonade instead of using the straw, which evidently is only for tornado-making. The straw bumps his nose and the bridge of his glasses.

"Cool," Derren says, flat and dry again.

There is more silence. The new band has also

finished, and chatter dominates the bar.

Derren and Anna get a cab. Jamie and Correy walk. Correy watches him fumble to get coins back in his wallet after leaving a tip on the bar. Derren had forgotten his wallet at home. Eventually, Jamie gives up on the wallet and shoves the coins into his pocket. As he and Correy walk, one quarter falls out. Correy hears it fall, but Jamie doesn't. She doesn't point it out or pick it up. She leaves it there on the sidewalk, shining under the streetlight like a miniature moon or the 'O' in a neon 'Open' sign, depending on the species of the viewer.

Tonight, Correy has the bathroom to herself. The lighting is cool, white, and harsh, emanating primarily from a circular makeup mirror. It is round and smooth. She touches her own face in it like she's in a trance. The skin of her reflection is cool and smooth. With her other hand, she touches her flesh face. It is warm and not smooth. She can feel dryness and scabs and thin fur along her cheeks.

Her face wash is an unscented one. She has considered purchasing a new one, with a nice scent, something fruity, like apricot or strawberry. In the stores though, she couldn't decide, so she went with an unscented version in a white and green bottle. It contains small, sharp beads like desert dirt. It scrapes and catches the scabs and pulls them away from her face, leaving her clean and new. Some of the scratchy beads are stuck to her face, along her cheeks, and in her eyebrows when she rinses the soap off. She takes a towel and scrubs them off, too. She touches her real face again. It is cooler and smoother, the hairs are smushed against her face, slicked closer to her skin. She smells like nothing.

Now her hands look dirty against her face. She sighs, washing and scrubbing at them again. There is still dirt stuck beneath her nails. Where does it even come from? She hasn't dug or touched any dirt.

Maybe that's the wrong order. Maybe the dirt doesn't come from the outside world at all. Maybe it's born beneath her nails, spawning, and growing, and sticking in the small space. She destroys it, driving the tip of one nail underneath the others, pulling dust and grime out, and rinsing it into the drain of the sink. It looks better now.

There's a short stubble on her legs, but she'd showered that morning. It'd be a waste of water to shower again. Plus, according to her mother, too much shampoo will dry out the roots of her hair, making it stringy and breakable.

The shame that moves like a worm is chewing through the dirt of her guts. She picks up a razor she brought, rolls her pant legs up to the knees, and slathers her calves in shaving cream. It's not clean or close, razor burn bubbles along her skin. She moved onto her other leg, starting on the front and moving slowly, clockwise, shaving in strips.

"Shit," she says to no one when the razor catches along the back of her heel. She grabs it, applying pressure. It hurts an irrational amount. It's not a cut, more of a burn. It's pink and fleshy, not bleeding, just exposed. It stings.

She rubs at it, hoping to make the pain dissipate faster. It barely helps. She wiggles her ankle, relieved it still moves. Logically, she knows a plastic razor meant for shaving is not going to sever her Achilles tendon. But the sting makes her stupid.

A lot of things make her stupid. Fear, for instance.

Anger. Hunger.

She's definitely missed some spots, patches of hair will grow back imperfectly, unevenly, but she gives up.

She doesn't want to leave evidence behind or clog the sink. She rinses the razor in the shower, thinking that *that* drain would be more apt to handle the hairs she rinses away than the drain of the sink.

Then, she wipes the counter of any of her hair and blood. She cleans it more carefully than she'd cleaned the crime scene.

She picks up a comb, and runs it through her hair with a vengeance, pulling on knots and snarls where they've formed. Her scalp protests; she doesn't stop.

She thinks that maybe she looks nice. Looks human. She smiles in the mirror and her teeth are normal. She keeps smiling, pulling back her gums and inspecting the teeth at the back of her mouth. They are molars, flat and square with grooves designed to crush and chew plant matter, such as fruits, vegetables, and nuts.

I have omnivore teeth, she thinks. She smiles in the mirror for a few seconds more.

Anna is back when Correy wakes, later than she usually would. She's still sleeping off alcohol and soda and her own reflection. Anna is talking with someone in a hushed but snippy voice, trying not to disturb her friend.

Please, don't let it be Derren, Correy thinks. She can only be polite to Derren in small doses, and she knows it's important to Anna that they all attempt to get along.

Then, Anna's conversation partner says something in an equally soft voice, plaintive and quiet.

It's not Derren. Derren's voice is perpetually stuck at a bad volume, except when he's insulting someone.

Derren would've just woken Correy up. It's not Derren, it's Jamie, Correy realizes. And she realizes if she shifts her head so that her ear is not smashed into the pillow, she can make out what they're talking, no, *arguing* about.

"...not nice to you," Jamie is saying, "He's not nice to anyone."

"You just don't know him like I do," Anna says. "I swear, he's not normally like that. He's normally very sweet. You have to get to know him."

"I do know him!" Jamie's voice gets louder, a fact he seems to notice immediately, and he drags it back down to a murmur. "Or at least, I know *a* version of him. A *bad* version. And if he's ever that version of himself with you, then he's not a good boyfriend."

"He's just stressed. He took on an internship lately in addition to his classes, which means he doesn't get as much sleep, which makes him grumpy and have less of a filter. That's all."

Jamie makes a breathy noise of frustration, part sigh and part squeal. "Having less of a filter isn't a free ticket to just be *mean*," he says.

"*Besides*," Anna hisses in return. "I'm an adult, and I can make my own choices. You respect me and you trust me enough to make my own choices, don't you?"

"Of course I do," he says, so softly that Correy has to lift her head the rest of the way to hear him. "Of course I do, but–"

"No 'but's. I love him."

"Okay."

"Thank you. I'm gonna go see if Correy's awake."

At the mention of her name, Correy re-buries herself in the blankets and pillows, trying to regulate her breathing back to the normal patterns of sleep. She squeezes her eyes shut.

She hears the doorknob turn.

"Correy?" Anna asks. "Hey, are you up?"

Correy makes a vague, sleepy sound of affirmation and lifts her head for the second time that morning. She rubs her eyes.

"What's up?" Correy asks.

"I was thinking about getting my nails done today," Anna holds out one of her hands for inspection. "One of mine got chipped last night. I want to get 'em redone. Not just a touch-up, but do something new. Maybe a color this time. Do you want to come with me?"

"Sure," Correy says, trying to make her voice sound as sleepy and normal and friendly as it should sound. "That sounds fun."

"Cool. Maybe we can grab some coffee on the way."

"Cool. Let me get dressed."

Correy stands and yawns, wider than might be normal, but better exaggerated than caught. She stretches, feels her spine pop, and gets ready in the mid-morning sun.

☾◯☽

Anna painted her nails a similar shade of red to her car. It lasts for six days before she chips the tip of her left pinkie finger.

"Again?" She sighs. "Damnit!" Anna is reading a psychology textbook when she notices the chip.

"What happened?" Correy asks.

Anna presents her hand instead of explaining; she lets Correy examine the spot where the red is missing.

"That's a bummer," Correy agrees. "Do you think you're going to have to get it redone?"

"Probably not. I hope not. It's small enough and close enough to the tip that I can probably just file it down and no one will notice," she examines them closely, then shifts her psych book off of her lap without closing it. "Actually, I'm just gonna do that right now."

She stands to go grab her nail file when there is a sharp knock on the door. Both freeze.

"Police!" Someone shouts on the other side. "Open up!"

"Shit," Anna whispers.

"Shit," Correy echoes. Her stomach feels as though it has run, thrown itself out of her body and out the window to escape, but it has left the rest of her body here, still and gutless.

"One second!" Anna says, her eyes flick around the space. She fusses with her hair, and half jogs to the door. Her eyes linger on her nail polish chip where it lingers on her hand which lingers in turn on the doorknob. She is maintaining the illusion of a normal college girl with nothing to hide.

Correy is frozen like a dumb animal, her only hope is that no one notices her.

Anna swallows and opens the door. Correy's throat contracts and she stays where she is.

"Afternoon, officers," Anna's voice is tight. "Is there a problem?"

The officers are two men with light brown hair shorn close to their scalps. They could be brothers; they are definitely members of the same species. Their uniforms are a dark blue, so dark they could almost be black. Detergent mixed with oil. No neon, no sky.

"No, no problem," one officer says. His badge number is 717. He continues. "We're just here investigating the disappearances of Tyler Bridges and Colton Klein."

"Oh, I'd read about that. So terrible!" Anna smiles, her jaw tight and too many of her teeth bared for it to be her real smile. Correy knows the feeling; she has not moved or spoken. She may not even be breathing.

"Terrible," 717 agrees. "Now, we're speaking to some of the people who may have seen them last.

Their last known location was at a party, at Beta Kappa. Some of your peers have placed you at that party. We're just asking everyone who was there some questions. Just part of the procedure."

"That makes sense," Anna says, breathless and nervous. "Would you like coffee?"

"We won't be questioning you here," the other officer, whose number is 4629 states. "We'll have to take you down to the station to question you. Separately.

"Just part of the procedure."

They did not let Correy and Anna take Anna's red car to the station. They piled them both into the back of a black and white police van with no windows in the backseat. It made Correy carsick.

She is still fighting nausea as she sits in the interrogation room. Both officers are with her: 717 stands in front of her, taking up her entire view. He smells like sweat. She probably smells like sweat as well. Cold, fear, sweat. Stomachless sweat. Can he smell her as well as she can smell him? Behind her is 4629, who stands near the door. She is not handcuffed to anything, but she imagines he is there to stop her from bolting. Anna is on the other side of the door, awaiting her turn to be questioned.

"There's nothing to be nervous about..." 717 starts to say.

"Am I under arrest?" Correy blurts out.

"No," 717 says. "This is just a routine questioning. We just want to know what you know. That's all."

"Okay. I don't know anything," she says, honestly.

4629 inhales behind her. She wonders if she's allowed to look behind her. She feels she isn't. All she can see is 717. He is all she can smell. Humanity can be so overwhelming. She thinks about running; she wonders if she could get past 4629; if they were smart they would have restrained her. Haven't they ever seen a werewolf movie?

"That's okay," 717 says, "We're still going to ask you some questions anyway. Did you attend the party at the Beta Kappa house at which Tyler Bridges and Colton Klein were last seen?"

"Yes."

"Did you notice anything strange at the party?"

"No," her throat tightens. "No. It was just a frat party. It was loud. And dark. And it kind of smelled bad."

Her breath leaves her lungs sharper and faster and louder than she means it to. She might be laughing; she might be panting. Maybe it's some new sound.

"Did you speak to Tyler or Colton that evening?"

"No, I don't think so." She strains to remember. Had she said anything to them? Has she just growled? Or exhaled in panicked little bursts, like she is now? She thinks she might've said something. "I might've said hello when we got there. But not a lot."

"Okay," 717 jots something on a notepad. "Last question: can you think of anyone who might've wanted to harm Tyler Bridges and Colton Klein?"

I wanted to, she thinks. *I was scared, and I was scared and I was so angry. And I was hungry.*

She did hurt at least one of them. One is still missing for her, too. But he hasn't gone to the police to tell them what happened. Scared? Of her? If Colten Klein went to the police and they asked him *how* or *why*, what would he say? Would he lie?

Her stomach has snuck past 4629 at the door and back into her body. It has taken residence at the hinge of her jaw, holding her teeth so close together the friction gives Correy a headache. It fills her mouth with the taste of bile and blood and rage; it has her by the tongue. She bites herself to stop it.

"You think somebody killed them?"

"It's a possibility," 4629 mutters behind her.

"Though an unlikely one," 717 says. Humans tend to confuse the body language for fear with the body language for anger. Perhaps the inverse is also true. 717 is speaking to her softly like he's trying to console her. "These were good people, no criminal records, many of the people we've spoken to have been their close friends. We have no reason to suspect anything of that nature... but when people have been missing for this long... It never hurts to ask the questions."

A missing person is presumed dead after seven years. Correy knows because she looked it up; she wanted to know who would give up first: the police or the earthworms.

"No. I can't think of anyone," she lies.

"Okay. Well, if you think of anything else, don't hesitate to call it in, okay?"

Correy just nods, no longer trusting her tongue, which is still under the control of her stomach. 4629 opens the door for her. He, too, smells like sweat. She doesn't look at him, but she feels him looking at her. She hears 717 lean back in his chair, sighing.

"Bring the other one in," he says with a rough sigh as the door starts to close behind her.

She has, evidently, been a frustrating animal.

Correy is not sure how long her own questioning had taken, but she thinks that Anna has been in there longer than she was. The clock in the precinct ticks constantly, unendingly. She attempts to count ticks, gets to 100, and gives up. Anna knew less, Anna was a better liar. There was no reason to assume she was spilling her guts right now. Yet, Anna and 717 and 4629 have one fundamental thing in common. Correy squeezes her eyes shut and hopes they won't appeal to Anna's sense of humanity. That'd be the end of it for Correy. She tries to count the ticking again and gives up again after 40.

Anna had said they'd go down together. She has to have some faith in that. She has to believe in her. She wrings her hands and fiddles with her nails in her lap. She had gotten white French tips when she and Anna had gotten them done together. The white hides the dirt that keeps reappearing; it looks nice, even though her nails are a little too short for the effect to look as elegant as it does on Anna. Anna is still in the interrogation room.

Can you think of anyone who might've wanted to harm Tyler Bridges and Colton Klein? It isn't that she *wanted* to harm anyone. She'd had to harm them. Where's the distinction? Had she wanted to? She cracks her knuckles and listens to them pop. What had she wanted? The corpse of Tyler Bridges had been mauled; even Jamie said that it looked like an animal. Do animals want to harm anyone?

There's a holding cell across the room from where Correy waits for Anna's interrogation. Two men and a woman sit in a cage. The woman is sitting on the ground with her knees up to her chest. She is silent. The two men sit on the bench, talking to each other in low voices. Correy wonders what they did to end up here; she wonders where the human fondness for cages has come from.

She counts 15 more clock ticks and gives up again. She strains her ears to listen for what Anna might be saying to the officers. She can't hear anything, not even indistinct murmuring. There's just the hum of the incandescent lighting and the clock ticks which go uncounted. Maybe they're talking about what a horrible thing has happened, wondering how a human being could make two other humans go missing. She can picture Anna's tight yet agreeable smile. Anna knows something they don't know. She promised if they went down, they would go down together, and they'd be roomies in prison still.

How much does Colton Klein know? How good of a glimpse of her face had he gotten? She remembers bodies close to her, but it had been so dark. Had he seen her face? The flash in her eyes? Had he bothered to look at her face? Or her teeth? Could he, if he came to the station, point her out in a crowd?

Correy wonders what she's most recognizable as, the human, or the canine.

Probably the human. Humans pay more attention to the distinct features of other humans. The canine stands out because it shouldn't be there, not because of anything it is. Humans pay attention to other humans.

Three more clock ticks. *If we go down, we go down together.*

Her attention drifts back to the humans in the cage. *I hope they robbed a natural history museum,* Correy thinks. The woman has uncurled herself and half-heartedly joined the conversation. *I hope they stole a dinosaur bone and buried it somewhere it doesn't go. I hope they're talking about what kind of bone to steal next, I hope the woman is voting to take a rib. Guy 1 thinks it should be a hip. Guy 2 thinks they should give up on bones and start taking the scale models out of the astronomy wing.*

Her stomach wonders which human would get eaten first if all three of them were to be left in that cage for eternity.

4629 opens the door again; Anna steps out.

Officer 717 offers to drive them back to their dorms in the squad car. Correy requests they walk, and Anna agrees.

"I think that went okay," Anna says when the police

station is out of sight.

"I think so too," Correy agrees, not certain she's being honest.

They walk home together in silence; they have both had enough of questions and answers.

Jamie wants to know in excruciating detail what they told the police officers so that if he is ever questioned, all of their stories will match.

"Why would they question you? You weren't there that night. You don't have any connection to this at all. You're fine," Anna sounds equal parts frustrated and comforting. She has a blister on the back of her heel, but neither of them wanted to get a taxi.

"You're right, but just in case. What did you tell them?"

"Nothing! That we went to a frat party. That it was a party full of cheap beer, and it was kinda lame and I left early. That's all."

Anna hadn't spilled her guts; it's a win for interspecies friendships.

"What about you?" Jamie asks Correy.

"No, nothing. Nothing interesting. I told them it was dark, I was drunk. I wasn't even sure if I had actually spoken to them that night. The officers asked me if I knew anyone who might want to hurt them. I said no. There are two that are missing, though. I don't know where the other one is. I think he's hiding. From me."

"Two? Missing?" Jamie asks. "See! This is why I ask! Do you think he saw you?"

Correy closes her eyes and sees teeth, grinning and biting. "I don't remember," she admits.

Jamie nods, less like he's agreeing and more like he's

gearing up to ask another question.

"But!" Anna interrupts. "The other guy–"

"Colton," Jamie says.

"–Hasn't gone to the police yet, for *whatever* reason. He probably won't ever go to them. What's he gonna say? He watched a girl overpower and kill his friend with her bare hands?"

Correy flinches and her mouth fills with saliva. *And teeth*, she thinks.

"Sorry, too much detail," Anna admits. "But my point still stands, if Colton was going to go to the cops, he would've already."

"You make a good point..." Jamey chews at his shakey fingernails. "Do you think anyone else saw you?"

"Haven't we had enough interoga–" Anna starts, at the same time Correy says, "No. No one else."

"You're sure? Because it seems like they're asking everyone who was at the party. Which is... weirdly thorough. I know when my bike got stolen–"

"–I think the parents have some sway with the cops," Anna says. "One of the officers kept mentioning how much the families missed them. Like, an uncomfortable amount."

Correy feels a high, whiney keen escape her throat.

"This is never gonna be over," she says. "I'm gonna go to jail if they don't send me to... I don't know.. Area 51 to do experiments."

"Hey. Don't say that," Anna says. "We're going to be fine," her voice is tight and has that shake to it.

"We were smart," Jamie agrees. "And it sounds like you held up really well. Cops don't suspect a thing. No one's going to Area 51," he nods his head as he says and rubs his hand along the back of his neck. They're comforting themselves as much as they're comforting her. Correy can smell the fear sweat on them, almost as strong as she smells it on herself.

She swallows and bites at her lips. They're dry and bleeding. She'll need to borrow Anna's red lipgloss or the mint-scented beeswax chapstick Jamie uses.

"Everything will be okay," she forces herself to say.

Correy is on a hunt. She sneaks onto the strip of poorly maintained grass that lines the back of the Beta Kappa house. She's camped behind the thick trunk of an orange tree, knees in the grass and surrounded by rotting fruit. It's a wonder the tree survives; it's dry for oranges, and it is getting cold enough that it's strange that the tree is still producing fruit. Nonetheless, the leaves above her head are still green, they share the branches with miniature suns. They must water it a lot and force it to produce.

From here, she can see the back door she vaguely recalls trying to leave through. From that spot, there are a few places one can run. Back into the house, but Colton would've had to push past her. Would she have allowed it? Probably not, not like that. He couldn't have run around the house and onto the street, for the same reasons. She would have chased him down.

That leaves running toward the orange tree, running toward the poorly maintained swimming pool, which is currently uncovered and full of leaves, or running up the hill. On the other side of the orange tree is the fence, then the sidewalk, then the street. On the other side of the pool is another fence, and then the yard area of another frat house.

The hill marks the transition between the frat backyard and the desert wilderness. The grass tapers off at its bottom, getting shorter and drier until it is dust and dirt. There had once been a fence, marking the official end, but it was knocked down and never put back up. At the top of the hill, there are scraggly trees and large rocks. Beyond the hill, there is an endless stretch of the same, occasionally crisscrossed by roads lined with churches, sun-baked convenience stores, and cheaper houses. Correy had woken up at the top of the hill.

Colton would've gone for the orange tree or the pool. He wouldn't take his chance with the desert, and *she* wouldn't have taken his dead friend in the same direction he ran. The fences can be jumped by a human; Correy knows because she, while roughly human-shaped, had jumped the fence to access her spot behind the orange tree.

She isn't sure what she's looking for. Footprints, scent, and trace had been buried by now, even if she were a better tracker. She had kind of been hoping he would still be here, crouched where he'd initially started hiding. She'd find him, then what? She'd finish the job? Bury him by his friend?

Just to see, she adjusts her position, raising her head toward the sky. She's listening. She breathes deep. It smells and sounds like a desert. This was a waste of time. She adjusts again and squashes a fat, half-decayed orange beneath her hand. It sprays her with juice and fruit flesh; its viscera clings to her skin. It's disgusting. She shakes herself to dislodge it with little success.

She feels worse about what she's done to that orange than what she did the last time she was here.

"I know it was kind of awkward last time," Anna says. "But some of Derren's friends are going tailgating before the game. He wants me to come. I don't always get along super well with his friends so I want you to be there. So I'm not as outnumbered."

Correy sighs. She doesn't want to go, but she goes where Anna goes, usually.

"Is Jamie going?" She asks.

"I don't know," Anna confesses. "I haven't asked him yet. He's probably going to say no. But I want him there too."

Correy nods. "Do you want me to ask Jamie?"

"You might have better luck."

"I'll ask."

)O(

Convincing Jamie takes their full, combined power. Eventually, he caved and joined them where they stand now, leaning against a white pickup truck that belongs to one of Derren's friends in the parking lot near the stadium. It's one of the cooler afternoons they've had so far. The scent of grilled meat fills the air, smokey, sweet, and heavy. Everyone is drinking, including Derren.

"Jamie! Drink?" One of the gaggle asks.

Jamie shakes his head.

"You were fuckin' right," the guy who asked says over his shoulder to Derren.

"I told you!" Derren says. He wraps his arms around Anna's waist and pulls her closer to him. He's sitting in the truck bed. Anna has her head on his shoulder. She is also sipping at a beer, albeit half-heartedly.

"Be nice," she says softly.

"I am!" Derren insists; he kisses the top of Anna's forehead. Derren is wearing a blue and white jersey, a display of team spirit. "Aren't I being nice, Jamie?"

"Sure," Jamie says.

The guy who offered Jamie a drink gestures at her, open beer bottle in hand. "You look familiar," he says, "Do I know you from somewhere?"

"I hang out with Anna a lot," she says, "And Jamie."

"Nah, it's not that," he says, "Something else. Party? Phi Delta? Beta Kappa?"

"That sounds familiar. Maybe some time, I did."

"Nice," he says. "Beta Kappa forever man, we get crazy."

"I didn't know you knew Derren."

"Everybody knows Derren, Derren's the best."

Derren is nibbling on Anna's earlobe. He has taken the partially finished beer bottle out of Anna's hands and is drinking from it in long gulps.

"Yeah..." Correy says. It's all she can think to say.

Another pickup truck pulls up, silver this time; it has a keg of cheap-smelling beer in the back that the driver hauls out proudly. He has a chip missing from one of his front two teeth.

Derren's assembled friends whoop and cheer at the arrival of the silver truck and the alcohol it contains. Derren himself is also enthralled, he stands from where he'd been sitting with Anna, whose arm snaps out to catch herself from tipping over, now that Derren has removed the shoulder she'd been leaning on. She glances around, to see if anyone noticed. Derren and his friends are helping to unload the keg. Jamie is squinting unhappily at the sun. Only Correy noticed, so she pretends she didn't.

"Jamie!" Shouts the guy from Beta Kappa Correy had spoken to earlier. Jamie jolts.

"What?" His eyes are wide, his pupils tiny from looking into the sun. He takes his glasses off to clean them on his shirt.

"Do you know how to do a keg stand?"

"No. No, I don't."

"Do you wanna learn?"

"I'm okay. Thank you though," he says, placing the glasses back on the bridge of his nose.

Correy sits beside Anna on the truck bed, on the opposite side of the empty space she imagines her friend is saving for Derren.

"This isn't going to end well," Correy whispers.

"No, no it's not," Anna agrees. Then louder she calls, "Hey guys! Leave him alone. If he doesn't want to, don't make him."

Jamie glances at her, silent gratitude twisting his mouth into the ghost of a smile.

Beta Kappa ignores her, "Come on," he insists, "Think of it like an induction ritual. If you want to hang out with us."

"I don't..."

Another guy, dressed in white and blue for team spirit interrupts again, "Do it!"

"Guys..." Anna says again, more insistently.

Derren sits back down, filling the space Anna has left for him. He drapes his arm around Anna's shoulders again, heavy, smelling of beer and sweat and meat.

"They're just havin' fun," Derren says. "Just chill, babe. Lay off."

Anna falls into a tense silence, squirming like she's trying to get more comfortable.

Another guy, in white and blue, has joined the group trying to coax Jamie. The colors do serve their purpose: they all look like members of the same species.

Blue-and-white knocks his shoulder into Jamie and white-and-blue laughs. Beta Kappa has put a mechanism that looks like a complicated garden hose or part of a car's engine onto the keg.

Jamie glances at Anna again. Anna looks away from him. His gaze turns to Correy, grim acceptance flooding his face.

"Fine."

More cheering from white-and-blue and blue-and-white and Beta Kappa. Derren laughs and makes a noise like a poor imitation of a dog barking; it sets Correy's teeth on edge.

A keg stand is a technique for consuming alcohol at parties wherein two to three people hold another upside down over a keg (a large, cylindrical container of alcohol, usually beer). It is an endurance exercise, to see how much liquid you can force into a human stomach in an awkward position for an awkward amount of time.

Correy's mother had made her promise before she left for college that she would never do a keg stand, because, as she had said, only tacky and tasteless women did them. It was an easy promise for Correy to make, seeing as she did not want to do one, ever.

She doesn't particularly want to watch Jamie do one, either; she looks away. Anna also looks away, so they end up looking both at the sky and at each other out of the corners of their eyes.

The sky is a pale, delicate blue that gets paler the closer it gets to the ground, a gradient going from robin's eggshell to chicken's eggshell. The sun lights Anna's eyes up from within. Her irises jump around the whites of her eyes like they can't decide where in the expanse to rest. She glances at Correy, then away again. Correy glances away, as well. She picks an arbitrary, fluffy, white cloud and keeps her eyes very still on that.

She hears a choking, sputtering noise behind her and cheering. White-and-blue and blue-and-white and Beta Kappa are chanting, "One of us!" Over and over and over again.

Correy tears her eyes away from her cloud. Jamie is doubled over with his hands on his knees, glasses missing, white foam clinging to the corners of his lips and dripping down his chin. White-and-blue slaps him on the back, beaming. Jamie doesn't look up at him, instead staggers a few feet off to the side and vomits on the asphalt, the same pale off-white as the sky where it meets the dirt.

"Jamie!" Anna cries, jumping off the truck bed and jogging to put a hand between her friend's shoulder blades as he vomits his guts up.

Correy would join, wanting to help, but she's frozen. She's also a sympathy vomiter, so perhaps it's for the best.

Derren shifts into the space Anna has abandoned. She inches away from him, throat tight with bile of her own.

"Your friend is a pussy," Derren says, taking a swig of his beer.

Her teeth tighten. "He's not," she says. "Your friends are assholes."

"They're just having fun," he says.

Correy stands, sharp and jagged and angry. She is in equal danger of vomiting, she realizes, whether she stays sitting where she is or goes to help her friends.

"You know," Derren says suddenly, as Correy turns to face him, she realizes his eyes are low, yet not at the ground. The urge to be sick roils again. He doesn't look at her face even as she looks at him. "You'd be really hot if you tried a little harder."

Correy says nothing to that and walks away, trying to get out of his line of sight as quickly as possible.

She finds Jamie's glasses near the keg. There's a spidery crack in the left lens. She picks them up and carries them to where Jamie is wiping his mouth with the back of his hand.

"Here," she says.

"Thanks."

"We should go," Anna says, "I'm sorry I dragged you guys here." Louder she repeats, "Hey guys! We're heading out!"

"Wait, you're leaving?" Derren has left the truck

bed. "Why? We're just having fun."

"It's not fun, it's—"

"You know you're being a total bitch right now, right?"

Anna shrinks, her voice going quieter. "We'll talk about this later," she says.

Derren scoffs, finishes what is at least his second beer, most likely his third or fourth, and returns to his truck bed, breath sour and footsteps angry.

They leave; the whole way back to the dorms, Anna is muttering "I'm sorry," under her breath. Over and over and over.

In the days between the tailgating party and the next full moon, Correy has constant, unrelenting nausea. Her organs feel twisted in on each other and contorted, aching, and tight. Her stomach is at the center, stretched and squeezed and surrounded by the rest of the mess inside.

"Do you think you've got some sort of stomach bug?" Anna asks when she complains.

"I don't think so," she says. "No fever."

She calls her mother, who suggests food poisoning.

She asks Jamie, who asks if it might be guilt.

She cuts her tongue on her canines on the morning of the full moon and thinks that he might be right.

The moon. She watches. Her eye is wide, open, and still. Like a quarter. The air is still. Full of smells. Leaves in their last moments on the tree. Dirt. Rabbits. Rotting oranges.

She is running. She is free. Her legs pass over dirt.

Free. Something is stuck to her foot. Something is stuck in her throat. Hurts. Sharp. Sticky.

She removes the sticker from her foot with her tongue. There is a small ladybug of blood where the thorn was. She licks it away, too. Better. *Tribulus terrestris*; denied. Plants stick to the fur of animals to be planted elsewhere. They should hurt less if that's what they want.

What is stuck in her throat is still stuck there.

Keeps running. More dirt. No thorns. The moon above her remains the same. The ground beneath her changes. Smooth, cool, pale. Made for humans. No thorns.

Growling. In the distance. No. Not growling, murmuring. Talking. In the distance. Lights. Eyes, twin moons. Approaching her. Metal, red, she thinks. Can't see red (too dark, wrong eyes). But knows it's red. Knows *its* red.

Friend!

Running again, chasing. Red metal is faster than her. Impossibly fast. Humans. Humans, who want so badly to go faster than humanly possible.

She is only as fast as her body allows. She has probably been faster before, when something wasn't stuck in her throat, crawling towards her mouth.

Red stops. More red, glowing in the sky. Like stars. More moons.

She stops as well. Waits. Waiting.

Red metal starts moving again. The red moons have changed. Green, now. She thinks. Can be hard to tell.

She knows her friend. She knows. She follows. Knows *that* red.

No new lights, but the red metal slows, turns toward the paler, smooth earth. Stops.

"Correy?"

Red door opens. Friend!

"What're you doing?"

Cannot speak, cannot smile. Feels joy throughout her body, can't show it.

"I know I said I wouldn't be back to the dorms tonight. But, uh... things change."

She twists her head. Unsure.

"I'm headed back now. Do you want a ride?"

No. *Canidae* unsatisfied. Night air sweet. Not yet. Runs, back onto pale asphalt, back to dirt.

"Okay? Bye?!"

She has left her friend. Considers going back. No, still want to run. Bring her with? No. Hunger twists her stomach and whatever is in her throat. Mild though. Ignorable. Still running.

Not just hunger. Something more. Something in the stomach. Not emptiness. Not meat. Strange.

Twisting more.

Wind stronger.

Cold.

Running. Twisting.

More running. More twisting. Sharper, tighter. Higher in the throat. Closer to the jaw. She's drooling.

Pauses near a small evergreen. Dark. Branches a darker dark against the dark. Something in her throat has come loose. In her mouth now. She retches. Drool comes with it, smooth and shiny.

Better.

Something sharp and white lies in the dirt.

The sun is rising. The moon retreats.

Correy wakes to the sound of birdsong and no dead bodies. She shifts, leaning to the side, and comes face to face with her own vomit.

There are better ways to wake up but it could be worse. Her head hurts, probably from dehydration, but nothing else does. A successful full moon. She shifts onto all fours to mitigate any dizziness before she stands all the way up. It's while her head is adjusting to the change in altitude and species that she notices the bone gleaming up at her from her puddle of puke.

Shoving squeamishness aside (it's all because of her, why should it make her nauseous? Any of it?) she picks it out. She stands the rest of the way, turning it over in her palm, holding it out to the sun. What do you think? She asks in her head. The sun doesn't answer her. The bone is small and delicate, a little piece of a larger, more complex, and more flexible structure. That larger, more complex, and more flexible structure is then attached again to *another* somehow larger, somehow more complex, and more flexible structure. It makes Correy's head spin. She probably bit *off* some part of Tyler, when she was mindlessly tearing him apart. Then she hadn't been able to digest it, so it just stayed within her. She might throw up again. She closes her hand around the bone and feels its pores absorbing the clamminess of her palm.

She should bury it.

That's the right thing to do, after all. And the smart thing. She walks out of view of her vomit puddle and scratches a small hole in the earth with her foot, dragging it through dry dirt over and over until she leaves a scar. She has to bury this bone. Now, it has both her genetics and the genetics of Tyler and herself. It linked her to him inescapably. The safest thing, really the only thing Correy can do is drop the bone into the hole she dug. She turns it over again in her hand, this strange little pearl of hers.

So *why* hasn't she dropped it yet?

What if someone digs it up? She asks herself. *What if some misguided soul decides to try to start a garden in the desert and when they dig to plant the tomato plants they find this human bone? They'll go to the police! And then what?*

So, *really* the safest place for it was to keep it with her. Where she could keep an eye on it. She closes the hole in the earth she'd opened, pulling the dirt back over it with the same foot. Too much of the dirt was upside-down; anyone could tell that someone had dug there. It's a good thing she didn't bury it. Someone would have found it for sure.

In her library, Correy tries to use the little bone as a paperweight, but she feels like she can see too many eyes on it. There's no one around her, Elizabeth from biology couldn't study with her today, so in Correy's little corner of the library, there was just her, and the bone. She still couldn't shake it, that feeling of being watched. She snatches it off of the table and closes her hand around it again.

The bone is not a suitable bookmark either. Correy thought that idea had some promise, but she was wrong. It's flat enough that it can mark a page without stressing the spine too much and she can keep it with her without feeling as though there are strangers' eyes crawling all over all her bones, the ones inside of her as much as the one outside of her. But, when she'd tried to put the bone in the book and the book in her bag at the end of the day, she couldn't do it. What if it broke? It's so fragile; she couldn't stand it if it broke, leaving dust and guilt over everything she had.

It lasts comparatively longer sitting on her nightstand. It's there when she wakes up and there when she goes to sleep, an occasional reminder of a secret well kept. The only people who are ever in the dorm room are her, Anna, and Jamie. In a way then, it's *their* bone, not just *her* bone, which makes it all a little bit better.

"What's this?" Jamie asks one evening during his increasingly frequent visits. He's fiddling with their bone fragment with a confused yet admiring expression and Correy knows she won't be able to leave it on the nightstand for much longer. She's been lying to herself.

"Cool rock I found," she lies to Jamie.

"It's neat. Where'd you find it?"

Once, when Correy was younger, her father had a coworker who liked to hunt. He'd had Correy's whole family come over for a dinner party where they served pork roast and red wine to the adults and cola with cherry juice to her. Just off of the kitchen, he'd had a room full of dead animals and their bones which he called his "trophy room".

"Where'd you get these?" a younger Correy had asked, staring up at a set of deer antlers mounted on wood high above her head.

"Those?" He'd asked, following her eyes. Then he'd smiled, blunt and friendly and flat, "Hunted and mounted 'em myself. Pretty, aren't they?"

She nodded, though she disagreed. The trophy room had a window that faced the backyard and she couldn't help but picture another deer, an alive deer, wandering by and seeing its friend displayed like that and not understanding why, but understanding very well that it could be displayed just like that.

Her father's coworker had walked them around the room, smiling and recalling every hunt and misadventure that had led to every stuffed duck and bobcat skull and deer antler that decorated the room. He had been so eager to tell them, so *proud, so excited.*

Correy isn't excited by her bone; she's *comforted* by it, which means it doesn't go on the mantle.

"Can I see?" Anna asks.

Correy wants to say, *No. No, you can't,* but Jamie is handing it to her too quickly.

"Pretty," Anna says. "Cool texture."

"Yeah," Correy agrees. She holds her hand out in a gesture that she hopes clearly indicates that she'd like her rock/bone/trophy/companion back now, *please.*

Anna drops it into her hand and returns to her phone. Jamie's eyes are back on his computer.

Correy curls protectively around her closed hand.

She's trying again to bury the bone. She returns to the spot she'd attempted to bury it in before. It's harder to find this time, the wind has piled more right-side-up dirt over it, but it's there. She re-digs the hole, opening an old wound.

She holds the hand that holds the bone out over the hole.

She wants to drop it and bury it.

The bones of her hand refuse to uncurl. There are no muscles in her fingers that she could use to force them.

She doesn't even bother to refill the hole she's dug this time, just slips her hand that holds the bone into her pocket and walks away.

Correy is standing in front of the mirror holding the bone up to various parts of her body; she's trying to find where it would match. The very tip of the pinkie finger, maybe? She holds it up to her own hand for comparison, trying to see if it might fit.

Maybe it's not a whole bone, maybe it's just a fragment, a sliver of some whole. Maybe that's why it's so hard to get rid of because the rest of the bone is still in her, wedged in her belly, in her gizzard, and in her soul.

She doesn't know what to do with it, or where it's supposed to go.

It feels the best when it's in her pocket, so she slips it back and keeps it there like a lucky rabbit's foot.

ALSO OUT ON FAR WEST

SONNY VINCENT......Snake Pit Therapy

BRENT L. SMITH......Pipe Dreams on Pico

JOSEPH MATICK......The Baba Books

KURT EISENLOHR......Stab the Remote

KANSAS BOWLING......A Cuddly Toys Companion

KANSAS BOWLING & PARKER LOVE BOWLING......Prewritten Letters for Your Convenience

CRAIG DYER......Heavier Than a Death in the Family

PARKER LOVE BOWLING......Rhododendron, Rhododendron

JENNIFER ROBIN......You Only Bend Once with a Spoonful of Mercury

JOSEPH MATICK......Cherry Wagon

RICHARD CABUT......Disorderly Magic

NORMAN DOUGLAS......Love and the Fear of Love

ELIZABETH ELLEN......Estranged

JEFFREY WENGROFSKY......The Wolfboy of Rego Park

HAKON ADALSTEINSSON......Our Broken Land

A FAR WEST ANTHOLOGY......Pretty Obscure

LILY LADY......NDA

NIKOLA PEPERA......Lay Down & Get Lost

JACK SKELLEY......Myth Lab

PETER CROWLEY......Down at Max's

STEVE KRAKOW......A Mind Blown Is A Mind Shown

farwestpress.com

+1 (541) FAR-WEST

www.ingramcontent.com/pod-product-compliance
Lightning Source LLC
Chambersburg PA
CBHW061552310726
48972CB00008B/2717